D0466469

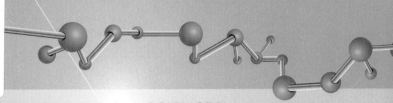

THE LIBRARY OF PHYSICAL SCIENCE™

Mixtures and Compounds

Marylou Morano Kjelle

The Rosen Publishing Group's

PowerKids Press™

New York

To my sister and friend, Francine Morano

Published in 2007 by The Rosen Publishing Group, Inc.
29 East 21st Street, New York, NY 10010

First Edition

Editors: Daryl Heller, Joanne Randolph, and Suzanne Slade
Book Design: Elana Davidian
Book Layout: Ginny Chu
Photo Researcher: Nicole Dimella

Photo Credits: Cover © Tony Freeman/Photo Edit; p. 4 © Brian Yarvin/Photo Researchers, Inc.; p. 5 © Philip Bailey/Corbis; p. 6 © Paul Edmondson/Corbis; p. 7 www.istockphoto.com/GJS; p. 9 © Kenneth Eward/BioGrafx/Photo Researchers, Inc.; p. 10 www.istockphoto.com/tmcnem; p. 11 © Michael Melford/Getty Images; p. 12 www.istockphoto.com/snaphappy; p. 13 © Lee F. Snyder/Photo Researchers, Inc.; p. 14 © Charles D. Winters/Photo Researchers, Inc.; p. 15 © Don Mason/Corbis; p. 16 © Jorg Nissen – StockFood Munich/StockFood America; p. 17 © George D. Lepp/Photo Researchers, Inc.; p. 18 © David Sailors/Corbis; p. 19 www.istockphoto.com/stinkyt; p. 20 © Anthony Cooper/Ecoscene/Corbis; p. 21 © Digital Vision.

Library of Congress Cataloging-in-Publication Data

Kjelle, Marylou Morano.
  Mixtures and compounds / Marylou Morano Kjelle.— 1st ed.
      p. cm. — (The library of physical science)
  Includes index.
  ISBN 1-4042-3420-9 (library binding) — ISBN 1-4042-2167-0 (pbk.)
  1. Mixtures—Juvenile literature. 2. Inorganic compounds—Juvenile literature. 3. Chemistry, Physical and theoretical—Juvenile literature. I. Title. II. Series.
QD541.K57 2007
541—dc22
                                                        2005032859

Manufactured in the United States of America

Contents

Physical and Chemical Properties

Every **substance** in the world is made up of atoms. Atoms are tiny bits of matter that combine to create everything from the blood inside our bodies to the lead in our pencils. Every substance also has a **unique** set of properties that we can use to describe it. There are two kinds of properties, physical and chemical. A physical property is something you can observe or measure. The color of your shirt, for example, is a physical property of that shirt. Shape, hardness,

Cooking an egg changes its physical properties. It cannot go back to being runny and clear, as an uncooked egg is.

and freezing, boiling, and melting points are other examples of physical properties. Whether a substance is a liquid, solid, or gas is another example of a physical property.

Chemical properties are how a substance acts under certain conditions. Wood's ability to burn, called flammability, is an example of a chemical property. Wood undergoes a chemical change as it burns. Once it becomes ash, it cannot go back to its original state.

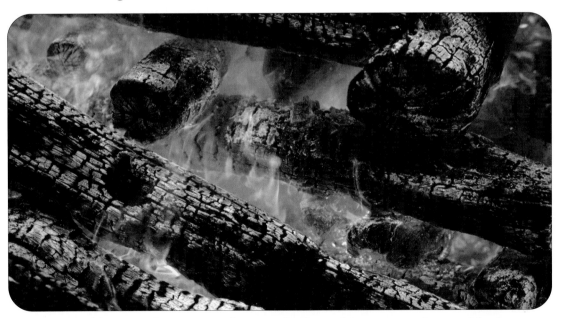

As wood burns it lets out carbon and other elements and turns black. This partly burned wood is called charcoal.

What Is a Mixture?

A mixture is created when two or more substances are combined. Mixtures can easily be separated again. The substances in a mixture do not **bond** together.

There are many types of mixtures. You can mix solids, such as sand and stones. You can also mix liquids, such as coffee and milk. Gases form mixtures with other gases, solids, or liquids.

Did you know that when you eat a bowl of chicken noodle soup, you

Sand and stones mixed together are a solid-solid mixture. Because the two parts of the mixture stay separate, this is a heterogeneous mixture.

are really eating a mixture? Chicken noodle soup is a **heterogeneous** mixture. This is because the noodles stay separate from the liquid. Sometimes you cannot see differences in a mixture because every part of the mixture is just like every other part. These mixtures are called **homogeneous** mixtures.

When coffee is mixed with milk, the two things combine in such a way that you cannot separate what is coffee and what is milk. This is an example of a homogeneous mixture.

What Is a Compound?

An element is something that cannot be broken down into a simpler substance. It is made up of atoms, just like everything else in the world. The gases hydrogen and oxygen are both elements. These elements combine to form a new substance called water. Water is a compound. A compound is a substance

H																	He
Li	Be											B	C	N	O	F	Ne
Na	Mg											Al	Si	P	S	Cl	Ar
K	Ca	Sc	Ti	V	Cr	Mn	Fe	Co	Ni	Cu	Zn	Ga	Ge	As	Se	Br	Kr
Rb	Sr	Y	Zr	Nb	Mo	Tc	Ru	Rh	Pd	Ag	Cd	In	Sn	Sb	Te	I	Xe
Cs	Ba	La	Hf	Ta	W	Re	Os	Ir	Pt	Au	Hg	Tl	Pb	Bi	Po	At	Rn
Fr	Ra	Ac	Rf	Db	Sg	Bh	Hs	Mt	Uun	Uuu	Uub	Uut	Uuq	Uup	Uuh	Uus	Uuo

	Ce	Pr	Nd	Pm	Sm	Eu	Gd	Tb	Dy	Ho	Er	Tm	Yb	Lu
	Th	Pa	U	Np	Pu	Am	Cm	Bk	Cf	Es	Fm	Md	No	Lr

There are more than 90 naturally occurring elements on Earth, plus many humanmade elements. These elements are listed on the periodic table, shown here. The table lists elements in rows and columns based on how alike their properties are.

that is made of different elements. The properties of a compound are not the same as the properties of its individual elements. Hydrogen and oxygen are both gases, but water is often a liquid.

The elements of a compound always combine in the same **proportion**. This means that every water molecule is the same as every other water molecule. Each water molecule is made of two parts hydrogen and one part oxygen.

Hydrogen

Oxygen

Hydrogen

A molecule of water is made from two hydrogen atoms and one oxygen atom.

There are 116 elements and about 23 million compounds that are known to exist right now. Scientists believe there are many more compounds yet to be discovered.

Solutions

If you **dissolve** a solid in a liquid, you will create a special mixture called a solution. For example, to make lemonade you dissolve sugar in water. After you have created a solution of sugar water, you can add lemon juice to make lemonade.

A solution is a homogeneous mixture. In a solution one substance is completely dissolved in another. For example, a milkshake is a solution. Ice cream is dissolved in the

Lemonade is a homogeneous mixture made from water, lemon juice, and sugar. Because everything is dissolved in a liquid, lemonade is a solution.

milk. Solutions can be made from liquids, solids, or gases. Soda is an example of a gas-liquid solution. Soda is a mixture of carbon dioxide gas and a flavored liquid. Brass is a solution of two solids, copper and zinc. Brass, copper, and zinc are metals.

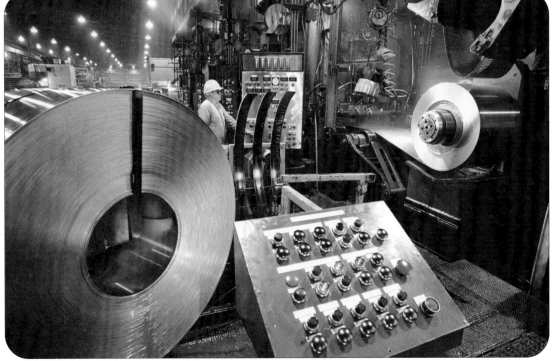

Brass is made in factories, such as the one shown here. The metals that make up brass are melted and combined. They are then allowed to cool back into a solid. Here the brass has been pressed into thin sheets.

Separating Mixtures by Size

Sometimes people want to separate mixtures back into their original parts. There are several ways to separate mixtures. A process, or method, known

Do you see the holes in this colander? The holes let the water pass through while keeping the beans inside the colander. This is how other filters work, too.

as filtration can take apart a mixture of a solid and a liquid. This method separates mixtures based on size, which is a physical property. A filter, which has small openings called pores, is used. Substances that are smaller than the pores pass through them. Substances that are larger get trapped in the filter.

Paper filters are used to make coffee, which is a mixture of ground coffee beans and water. The filter lets the smaller water and coffee molecules flow through its pores while it traps the larger coffee grains in the paper. A metal kitchen **colander** is another type of filter. You use a colander to separate spaghetti from the boiling water. The colander allows the cooking water to pass through it, but it holds the spaghetti back.

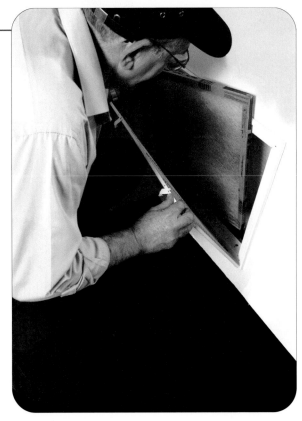

A worker is cleaning a filter from an air conditioner. The filter removes dirt and other substances from the air.

Separating Mixtures by Density

Density is a physical property that measures how close together the atoms of a substance are. Denser substances are heavier than those that are less dense. For example, air is not very dense, while a brick is quite dense.

Density can be used to separate the substances that make up a mixture, because each substance in

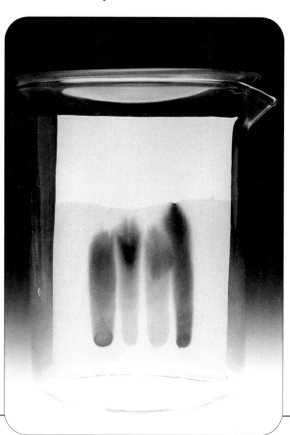

Chromatography is a way that scientists can separate mixtures back into their separate parts. The process can be used to separate colored dyes, pigments, and many other things. The materials that make up the substance separate at different rates and form bands, like the ones shown here.

a mixture has its own density. For example, if a mixture of sand and oil is placed in water, the sand will sink to the bottom of the **container**. The sand is more dense than the water. The oil will rise to the top of the water because it is less dense than water.

The rocks in this fishbowl are denser than water, so they sink to the bottom. The fish floats. Do you know why? Fish have something called a gas bladder. The gas bladder is filled with air. It lowers their density to make them lighter than the water.

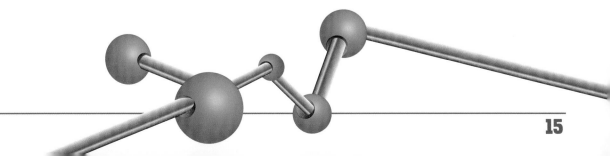

Separating Mixtures by Temperature

There are three states of matter. These states are liquid, solid, and gas. Substances, like water, can exist in all three states. When liquid water reaches its freezing point, it turns into ice. Ice is a solid. Ice will return to a liquid when it reaches its melting point. If liquid water is heated, it will turn into a gas when it reaches its boiling point.

Water can be seen in all three states in this picture. A stream of liquid water runs through ice and snow. The steam that can be seen is water vapor.

When sugar is mixed with water, it dissolves. When the solution is heated and then cooled, the sugar molecules stick together again and form large crystals. This is how rock candy is made.

Each substance has a different boiling point, melting point, and freezing point. Some mixtures can be separated using hot or cold **temperatures**. For example, a mixture of sugar and water can be separated by using heat. Heat will separate the water and sugar using a process called evaporation. During evaporation liquid water is turned into a gas. After the water is removed, large chunks of sugar are left. People use heat to separate sugar from a mixture of sugar water to make rock candy.

Compounds and Oxygen

Oxygen gas makes up 21 percent of Earth's **atmosphere**. Many substances **react** with oxygen gas. The ability to react with oxygen is an example of a chemical property. When substances react with each other, they change into a new substance with new properties. For

These cans have been left out in rain and other wet weather. This has caused rust to form on the cans. Rust is the flaky brown compound that can be seen on the cans.

example, if you leave your bike outside in the rain for a long time, its shiny metal might rust. When this happens, the metal turns brown and flakes, or peels off. The oxygen in the atmosphere combines with the water in the rain. The combination of oxygen and water causes some metal compounds to break down and rust.

Rusting is a chemical reaction. As other chemical reactions do, rusting creates a new compound. Rust is a compound scientists call ferric oxide. Not all compounds produce rust when oxygen is present. Plastics do not rust because they do not react chemically with oxygen.

The copper metal in the Statue of Liberty is not shiny anymore because copper reacts with oxygen. This reaction forms a green compound.

Compounds and Water

Combining something with water is called hydration. Hydration makes many new compounds. Cement is one compound that is made by hydration. Water is added to substances such as **limestone** and clay to make cement. Builders use cement to make blocks and stones stick to each other. When the wet cement dries, the blocks and stones are joined by the cement.

Here cement is being used to join bricks. Before it is mixed with water, cement is dry and powdery. Adding water causes it to form a sticky compound that then dries, binding the bricks together.

The entire ocean is a mixture. It is made from the compounds water and salt. The salt dissolves in the water. If the water evaporates, or becomes a gas, the salt is left behind.

Many compounds are soluble in water. This means they dissolve easily in it. Sodium chloride is the chemical name for table salt. Salt is soluble in water. When salt is added to water, the two elements that make up salt break away from each other. Each of these elements joins itself to part of the water molecule. You cannot see the tiny pieces of salt once they have dissolved in water.

Everyday Compounds and Mixtures

We use compounds and mixtures every day. Most of what you see around you is either a compound or a mixture. Everything we eat and drink is a compound or a mixture, too. The air we breathe is a mixture of oxygen, nitrogen, and other gases. Soil is a mixture of rock, minerals, and sand. The salty water in the ocean is a mixture of water and salt.

Some mixtures and compounds are synthetic. Synthetic mixtures and compounds are not found in nature, but are created by people. Glass, paint, and some plastics are examples of synthetic compounds and mixtures.

Synthetic mixtures and compounds make our lives easier and better. We need natural mixtures and compounds to eat, drink, breathe, and even bathe. The lives of everyone in the world depend on mixtures and compounds.

Glossary

atmosphere (AT-muh-sfeer) The gases around an object in space. On Earth, this is air.

bond (BOND) Join with or connect to.

colander (KAH-len-der) Something used for drawing off water from food.

container (kun-TAY-ner) Something that holds things.

dissolve (dih-ZOLV) To break down.

heterogeneous (heh-tuh-ruh-JEE-nee-us) Made up of many different things.

homogeneous (hoh-muh-JEE-nee-us) Made up of many things that are the same.

limestone (LYM-stohn) A kind of rock made of the bodies of small ocean animals.

proportion (pruh-POR-shun) The measure of one part compared to another.

react (ree-AKT) To act because something has happened.

substance (SUB-stans) Any matter that takes up space.

temperatures (TEM-pur-cherz) How hot or cold something is.

unique (yoo-NEEK) One of a kind.

Index

A
atoms, 4, 8, 14

B
boiling point, 5, 16

C
chemical properties,
4–5, 18

F
filtration, 12
freezing point, 5, 16

G
gas(es), 6, 8–9, 11,
16, 22

H
heterogeneous
mixture, 7
homogeneous
mixture, 7, 10
hydration, 20

L
liquid(s), 6, 9–12,
16

M
melting point, 5, 16
molecules, 9, 13, 21

P
physical properties,
4–5, 12

S
solid(s), 6, 11–12,
16
solution, 10–11

Web Sites

Due to the changing nature of Internet links, PowerKids Press has developed an online list of Web sites related to the subject of this book. This site is updated regularly. Please use this link to access the list:
www.powerkidslinks.com/lops/mixcomp/